READ
TO
ME
STORIES

Illustrated by
Eric Kincaid

BRIMAX BOOKS · CAMBRIDGE · ENGLAND

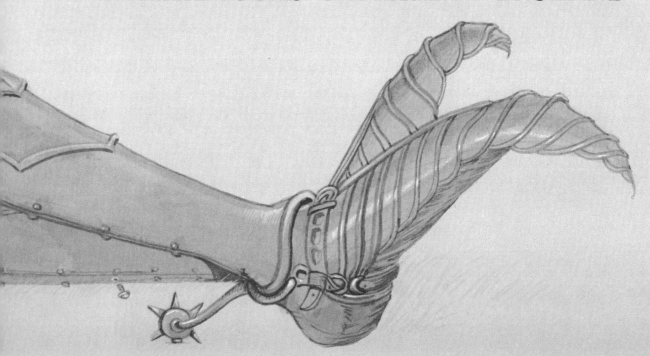

ISBN 0 86112 131 7
© BRIMAX RIGHTS LTD 1982 All rights reserved
Published by BRIMAX BOOKS, CAMBRIDGE, ENGLAND
Printed in Hong Kong

CONTENTS

THE PUMBLECHOKE ROCKET

Mr Pumblechoke was bored. He had cleaned his car, cut the lawn, dug the garden and put up a new shelf in his kitchen. His house was spick and span and his garden neat and tidy. That's why he was bored.

He sighed, and picked up a magazine. On the front cover there was a picture of a spaceship. A shiny, silver spaceship with hundreds of dials and levers and switches. Mr Pumblechoke was very interested in Space. In fact, he had written to the American President three times, asking if he could be an astronaut. But, each time he had received a polite reply, saying that old people were not allowed into Space. They might get dizzy.

After studying the picture for some time, Mr Pumblechoke had a brilliant idea. He decided to copy the picture and build his own spaceship in the back garden. He could go to the Moon all by himself!

In the weeks that followed, he didn't have time to be bored. He hammered and glued and polished and sprayed. Slowly, the shapeless heap of scrap metal began to look like a rocket. He made knobs out of cotton reels, stuck empty baked-bean cans together for the exhaust pipes and nailed a cuckoo clock inside so he could time his journey. He sprayed the whole rocket with silver paint and wrote ''The Pumblechoke Lunar Rocket'' on one side in red letters. It looked marvellous!

"I'm going to the Moon, Mrs Wobblethorpe!" he called to his
neighbour, "I'll bring you back some rock."

Mrs Wobblethorpe went quite pale when she saw the home-made
rocket.

"You go careful, Mr Pumblechoke," she said. "You're not getting any
younger, you know."

A large flowerpot covered with silver foil and two eye-holes and a mouth cut in it made a super space helmet. Then, Mr Pumblechoke carefully painted his old overalls and boots with silver paint. He packed some food and a map and decided to take off the next morning.

The alarm clock rang at five o'clock and Mr Pumblechoke leapt out of bed. He was so excited. He put on his space outfit and hurried downstairs for breakfast. He had to take off his space helmet, because he couldn't eat his cornflakes with it on. Then he rushed out to check the rocket's engines.

Everything was perfect! He looked up to check that there were no birds or planes flying overhead and pressed the ignition button. The engines fired and the rocket slowly and gracefully lifted into the air. Mr Pumblechoke beamed. "We have lift-off!" he said to himself.

As the rocket gained speed, Mr Pumblechoke watched from the window as the land grew smaller and smaller. He planned to be on the Moon by suppertime and he would have banana sandwiches and chocolate cake to celebrate.

He was just checking his food supply when the rocket suddenly turned to the left and hurtled on into the darkness. Mr Pumblechoke checked his map. This wasn't the way to the Moon. In fact, it was the way to nowhere!

Some hours later, Mr Pumblechoke, who was rather worried by this time, saw a bright light in the distance. He put on the brakes and started to slow down. The bright light became bigger and bigger.

"It must be a planet," he said to himself. He didn't know which one, but he decided to land anyway.

The rocket bumped down gently on the dusty surface.

Mr Pumblechoke opened the door and climbed down the steps. To his surprise, the rocket was surrounded by funny little people. They were very small with pointed noses and chins. They all had green curly hair and wore red spacesuits.

Mr Pumblechoke felt dizzy with shock. "Er, excuse me," he said, "I'm Mr Pumblechoke, Arnold Pumblechoke. Is this the Moon?"
The funny little people laughed, and one replied,

"He wants to know just where the Moon is
Doesn't he know that we're the Loonies?
Only in rhyme can we converse
We call our plant the Looniverse."

Mr Pumblechoke smiled. The Loonies led him to a large building. Inside, there were tables laden with food.

"After your meal, you come with us
A sight-seeing trip in our Looniverse bus," said a Loony.
Another pulled at his sleeve.

"I'm the bus driver. I am clever
Will you stay here forever and ever?'

Mr Pumblechoke explained that he was only taking a short trip, because he was bored at home.

The Loonies all crammed into the Loonibus and Mr Pumblechoke sat at the front. They trundled in and out of Loonicraters, up and down dried up Loonirivers and along dry, dusty Loonitracks until they had seen the whole of the Looniverse. There were also large Loonibeasts that lived in the Loonicaves. Mr Pumblechoke thought it was wonderful.

They all jumped out of the Loonibus and Mr Pumblechoke sat down quickly on a rock.

"If your head feels rather queer
It is our different atmosphere," said a Loony.

"We all felt like you at first
We thought our heads were going to burst," said another.

Mr Pumblechoke liked the Loonies very much, but he felt it was time he went home. The Loonies all crowded round him.

"Please say you'll stay and be our King
You will get used to everything," said one.

"No one ever comes to see us here
You are the first for many a year," said another.

Mr Pumblechoke shook his head. "My home is far away," he said. He thanked them all and shook hands with everyone. Then he climbed the steps of his rocket.

'Goodbye, everyone and thank you again. I should be home by half past ten," he said.

The Loonies cheered loudly and he realised he had spoken in rhyme.

The rocket door closed behind him and the engines burst into life once more. He waved until the Loonies were out of sight and set the engines at full speed for home.

The hours soon passed by and the cuckoo in the clock came out ten times. Mr Pumblechoke looked out of the window and could see land clearly, like a twinkling fairyland below him. He carefully steered the rocket down right over his back garden.

He crashed into a big leafy tree but luckily was not hurt. He felt very silly hanging from a branch by his trousers. He wriggled himself free and started to walk home. The silver foil was peeling from his helmet and the silver paint was flaking from his spacesuit. He was very glad everyone was in bed.

He arrived home, tired but happy. He opened the kitchen door and found Mrs Wobblethorpe waiting for him with a nice, hot drink.

"Welcome home," she said. Mr Pumblechoke sipped his drink.

"Next time I'm bored," he said, "I'll play a game of cards. That doesn't make me dizzy!"

MISS POLLYWOBBLE

Miss Pollywobble put another log on the fire and watched it blaze merrily away. It was a bitterly cold evening and Baggy, her ginger cat sat very close to the fire. Outside, the snow started to fall and by bedtime, the countryside was covered by a huge, white snowy blanket.

''We haven't many logs left,'' said Miss Pollywobble the next morning, as she gave Baggy his milk and sardines for breakfast. ''I've ordered some from the village. Maybe they will come today.''

Baggy purred happily and tucked into his food.

But the snow continued to fall steadily and almost covered the cottage. Miss Pollywobble and Baggy began to feel very cold. They had run out of logs and none could be delivered because the roads were blocked by snowdrifts.

Miss Pollywobble wore two dresses, three cardigans, a woolly hat and a pair of big, fur boots. She ate hot soup and toast and managed to keep warm. Baggy stopped purring altogether and shivered miserably. He snuggled up to Miss Pollywobble to keep warm.

''Poor Baggy,'' she said, cuddling him close to her. ''Let's find you a blanket.'' She opened the cupboard and out fell a big bag of wool.

After staring at it thoughtfully for some time she said, "I've just had the most marvellous idea, Baggy. I shall knit something to keep us both warm."

She found a large pair of knitting needles and made herself comfortable. All day and all night she clicked away as the knitting grew bigger and bigger. At last it was finished. It was enormous!

Baggy was very puzzled. He watched as Miss Pollywobble went outside carrying her largest broom. She pulled a ladder out from under the snow and climbed up onto the roof. Then she swept every bit of snow from the walls and roof until they were spotlessly clean. She then returned indoors to fetch the 'marvellous idea' and climbed the ladder again. With a few tugs and a few pulls the knitting fell into place.

Baggy blinked hard.

Miss Pollywobble had knitted a gigantic red tea cosy! It fitted the cottage perfectly. The hole for the handle was over the front door and the hole for the spout was over the back door. The chimney poked through the red pom-poms on the top.

It was a little dark inside the
cottage but it was beautifully warm.
Baggy snuggled down happily and
Miss Pollywobble took off her big,
fur boots. They were warm inside
their giant tea cosy and didn't mind
at all when it began to snow again.

It snowed steadily for days. One
morning, Miss Pollywobble woke up
to find the cottage strangely light
and extremely cold. She quickly
flung open the window.

"Baggy!" she cried, sadly. "Our
tea cosy! It's disappeared!"

Baggy shivered sadly. Miss Pollywobble looked hard at the
snow-covered countryside. Whoever had taken the giant tea cosy had
been very careful indeed! The snow was smooth and there were no
footprints. She closed the window thoughtfully and went downstairs.

She warmed some milk for Baggy's breakfast and made herself some
coffee. Birds twittered noisily on the window ledge. Miss Pollywobble
always gave them breadcrumbs for breakfast and she scattered a handful
from the window. As she did so, she saw something flapping gently in the
snowy hedge. It was an end of red wool!

"Come on, Baggy," she cried, pulling on her snow shoes. "We're going
to follow that wool!"

She put Baggy into her shopping basket and they set off. The red wool trailed over fields and farms and along narrow lanes. After many, many miles they came to a dark, gloomy forest. A square, wooden sign said,

KNITTINGHAM FOREST. KEEP OUT.

The trail of wool led deep into the forest and then stopped suddenly. Miss Pollywobble looked all around while Baggy started digging with his front paws and then jumped back in alarm.

He had found an old underground tunnel and the red wool continued along it.

Bravely Miss Pollywobble made her way into the tunnel and Baggy came slowly behind. It was damp and dark and silent. The wool led them on until they come to a big brown door. They could hear lots of squeaky voices chattering inside.

Miss Pollywobble took a deep breath and slowly opened the door.

Inside was a large, bright room full of small, elf-like creatures. They wore green, knitted clothes and all looked alike. The floor was covered with balls of wool and everyone was busy knitting with the tiniest needles Miss Pollywobble had ever seen. Everyone became very, very quiet.

"Please don't be afraid,' she said, gently. "I'm Miss Pollywobble, and this is my cat, Baggy. We followed the trail of red wool from our giant tea cosy. Please tell us who you are."

Then one of the elf-like creatures stepped forward.

"We are the Knit Wits," he said. "We live here in Knittingham Forest and spend all our time knitting."

21

"But what do you knit?" asked Miss Pollywobble. The Knit Wit led her across the room to some small drawers neatly stacked together. In the top drawer there were lots of tiny yellow, knitted tubes.

"In the very cold weather," explained the Knit Wit, "the catkins in the forest would freeze. We knit little covers to keep them warm."

Miss Pollywobble smiled. "What a lovely idea," she said.

The rest of the Knit Wits gathered round to show off their knitting. There were tiny red vests for the robins and pretty yellow hats for the daffodils, and long ear muffs for rabbits. There were bluebell covers and white snowdrop covers. In fact, every living thing in Knittingham Forest had something warm for the winter.

Miss Pollywobble liked the Knit Wits very much. "How kind you are," she said, gently.

One of them touched her arm. "We're so sorry we undid your giant tea cosy," he said, "but our red wool was stolen and we needed some new vests for the robins."

A loud tapping on the door made everyone jump.

"It's Colonel Crow!" cried the Knit Wits. "He's the one who stole all our red wool to make himself a warm nest. Quick, Miss Pollywobble, hide in the wool cupboard!"

The door suddenly burst open.
"We've no more wool for you,
Colonel Crow," said a Knit Wit. "If
you leave us alone we will knit you a
new nest. Please go away."

But the Crow took no notice and
started gathering wool from the
floor.

The Knit Wits huddled together in
a corner. Colonel Crow was the
nastiest Crow they had ever met and
they were very frightened.

Then, the door of the wool cupboard burst open with a crash and out
sprang Baggy, looking very angry. Colonel Crow, dropped all the wool
and with a startled "Caw" ran to the tunnel. Baggy chased him out into
the daylight and through Knittingham Forest. He made sure that Colonel
Crow flew far, far away.

The Knit Wits were delighted and thanked Baggy over and over again.
Miss Pollywobble picked him up and popped him in her basket once
more. Then she said goodbye to each Knit Wit and promised to visit them
again soon.

The sun was shining as they walked across the fields. The trees began to drip as the snow started to melt. When they arrived home they were happy to find their logs had arrived at last and were stacked neatly against the wall of the cottage. Baggy purred happily at the thought of a blazing log fire.

Some days later, Miss Pollywobble found a large brown paper parcel on the doorstep. She opened it very carefully and found a pink, knitted vest for herself and a ginger knitted coat for Baggy. She smiled fondly. She knew exactly who had sent them!

GOLD

There's gold in the meadows
And gold in the trees;
It shines on the buttercups,
It shimmers on leaves.
There are golden-eyed daisies
And marigolds to pluck;
Bright gold of the daffodils
Pale gold of the duck.

There's gold on the eagle
And small crested bird;
There are fine golden fishes
In thousands, I've heard.
There's gold that men dig for
Down in the earth;
Then bury in Banks
And count up its worth.

But listen, Great Sun,
As you sink in the west:
Your gold so warm
Is the loveliest.

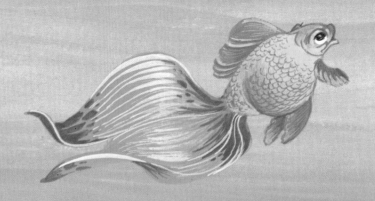

JASPER'S TRAVELS

"It should be lunch time by now," said Jasper the goldfish. He knew his friend Peter wasn't usually late feeding him, but it got rather boring sometimes just swimming round and round.

Jasper peered through the side of his bowl, and blinked crossly. He could see Peter and his mother and father eating their lunch.

"Just waiting and waiting," he went on. "I wish I could have a real adventure, but I have nowhere to go and nothing to do."

Just then Jasper felt his bowl being lifted high into the air, and carried along rather jerkily until he landed right next to the kitchen sink.

"Oh," gasped Jasper. "I suppose I've got to have my water changed now. I do hope the water is warm enough this time. Last week it was freezing. I had a chill for days – brrrr. Oh dear, and all this before lunch."

Peter was always very careful when he changed Jasper's water. He caught him first in a little fishing net, and popped him into a clean jar of water. Then he cleaned his bowl thoroughly and filled it with fresh water. Catching Jasper again in the little net, Peter carefully put him back into his bowl.

"My, that feels good," said Jasper and gave a wriggle of delight. "That feels very good," he said, and gave an even bigger wriggle.

Suddenly, with a jerk of his head, and with a flip of his tail, he jumped up and over the edge of his bowl, and into the sink. He wriggled towards a large round hole, and felt himself falling down, down, down. It was very dark.

"I must find some water soon," gasped Jasper.

Suddenly Jasper felt himself falling through into the bluest, cleanest water he had ever seen. All around him were beautiful plants and flowers, shells and stones, and tiny insects and grubs. Just then, a large grey fish with red spots swam by.

"Hello!" he called. "My name is Mr Plaice. Who are you?"

"I'm Jasper the goldfish," Jasper replied. "I'm lost. Where am I please?"

"Why," replied Mr Plaice. "You're in the sea of course. We don't get many goldfish in the sea. You'd better watch out for sharks and the whales. They're very large, and would find you very tasty."

Jasper shuddered. He didn't like the idea of being eaten for supper. He thought only people did that.

"Come with me," said Mr Plaice. "I'll take care of you."

Together they swam through the clear waters until they reached a large wooden object stuck in the sea bed.

"This is Fishville Colony," said Mr Plaice. "A large ship sank here many years ago, and we've made it our home. It gives us shelter when the sea is stormy and we can hide here safely if we know there is any danger around." All around swam the most beautiful fish Jasper had ever seen. Baby minnows darted swiftly between plants, and swam in and out of the timbers of the old ship. Everywhere he looked were fish of different shapes and sizes.

Jasper swam up and up, nibbling as he went at any small insects which came within his reach. A big round object with two large eyes and eight spindly legs floated towards him.

"Who are you?" gasped Jasper.

"I'm Octopus," replied the odd shape. "I need all my legs for catching my food as I cannot swim around as quickly as you can."

Jasper quickly darted away and swam on further.

Suddenly, Jasper felt himself being dragged forward. All around him now were lots of other fish all trying in vain to swim free. He felt himself being pulled up and up until, once again, he was without water, this time packed between a shoal of heaving and wriggling fish. He could hear voices, men's voices.

"Not a bad catch this time."

The fishermen heaved the net into the boat and looked over their catch.

"Why," said one, "if it isn't a goldfish! Never caught one of those before. Better put him back into the sea."

"No, wait," said another voice. "I'll take him to my brother's pet store. A fine looking fish like that should fetch a good price."

Jasper felt himself being plunged into a box of icy water, and the little fishing boat rocked from side to side making Jasper feel rather queer.

"Oh dear," he said. "Whoever heard of a goldfish feeling seasick."

Soon, the fishing boat was tied up, and the fisherman tucked the box under his arm, and set off for his brother's pet store.

Jasper closed his eyes sadly. How he longed to see his friend Peter again.

Inside the pet store the fisherman's brother looked down at Jasper.

"Ah yes, I'll soon sell this little fellow. Let me put him into the tank with the other goldfish."

Once again, Jasper felt himself sliding into different waters, only this time into a tank already overcrowded with tiny fish.

"Mind your manners," snapped a little goldfish with silver lines on his back, as Jasper bumped into him for the third time.

"I'm sorry," replied Jasper, "but I'm looking for some food. It seems ages since I last ate, and I'm very hungry."

"We've eaten it all," came the reply. "We never get enough in here. Too many fish and not enough food. That's the trouble here."

Jasper suddenly became aware of a man peering into the tank looking at all the fish one by one.

"I expect he likes me the best," thought Jasper excitedly, and darted and swam as cleverly as he could.

"Yes, I'll take the lot," said the man to the store owner. He handed over some money, and lifted the tank up and carried it out of the store into the back of a large red truck. Off they went, all the fish bumping into each other as the truck rounded corners, until they arrived at a large park.

"Roll up, roll up. Lots of fun and games for everyone."

Jasper heard lots of shouting as the tank was lifted out and onto the centre of a large round stall. He opened his eyes wide. All around, people were throwing hoops trying to catch them on hooks in front of the tank. Some of the hooks had numbers on them.

"Come and play Hoop-la," shouted the man. "Win a beautiful goldfish."

Jasper had never been to a fairground before, and didn't like it very much at all. He felt very lonely and afraid.

Just then, he heard a voice shout, "Oh, I've won! I've won a goldfish!"

"Well done, Peter," a voice replied. "Now choose which one you would like."

Jasper gave the biggest wriggle he could manage. He *knew* that voice. It was his friend Peter.

"Why, this one looks just like Jasper," exclaimed Peter. "Wait! It *is* Jasper. Look, he's so excited he's trying to tell me to choose him. Hello, Jasper old fellow, we'll soon have you home safe again."

Peter just couldn't understand how Jasper had arrived at the fairground. He'd felt very upset when he had lost him, and never expected to see him again.

A man put Jasper into a little bag with airholes in the top, and Peter carried him home. On the table where Jasper's bowl had stood was the biggest, shiniest fish tank he had ever seen.

"There," said Peter. "We bought this for you just before you disappeared. I shall put plants and rocks in it for you, and you'll be able to have much more fun."

Jasper smiled to himself as he swam through the clear water in his lovely new tank. It was wonderful to feel cosy and safe again and to have lots of food. As for his adventures, well, even a goldfish can dream sometimes.

WYNKEN, BLYNKEN, AND NOD

Wynken, Blynken, and Nod one night
   Sailed off in a wooden shoe, –
Sailed on a river of misty light
   Into a sea of dew.
"Where are you going, and what do you wish?"
   The old moon asked the three.
"We have come to fish for the herring-fish
   That live in the beautiful sea;
Nets of silver and gold have we,"
   Said Wynken,
      Blynken,
        And Nod.

The old moon laughed and sung a song,
   As they rocked in the wooden shoe;
And the wind that sped them all night long
   Ruffled the waves of dew;
The little stars were the herring-fish
   That lived in the beautiful sea.
"Now cast your nets wherever you wish,
   But never afeared are we!"
So cried the stars to the fisherman three,
      Wynken,
      Blynken,
        And Nod.

All night long their nets they threw
    For the fish in the twinkling foam,
Then down the sky came the wooden shoe,
    Bringing the fishermen home;
'Twas all so pretty a sail, it seemed
    As if it could not be;
And some folk thought 'twas a dream they dreamed
    Of sailing that beautiful sea;
But I shall name you the fishermen three;
        Wynken,
        Blynken,
        And Nod.

Wynken and Blynken are two little eyes,
    And Nod is a little head,
And the wooden shoe that sailed the skies
    Is a wee one's single bed!
So shut your eyes while Mother sings
    Of wonderful sights that be,
And you shall see the beautiful things
    As you rock on the misty sea
Where the old shoe rocked the fishermen three,
        Wynken,
        Blynken,
        And Nod.

FELIX THE MAGICIAN

Long, long ago there lived a good and clever magician whose name was Felix. He lived on the border between two warlike countries. Felix knew that King Lofty on the one side and King Trump on the other were jealous of each other and needed little excuse to start a war.

Their armies trained by marching up hill and down dale all day long. Tramp, tramp, tramp.

Felix was cross.

"I must put a stop to it," he said to himself. But how?

Felix thought and thought. He even worried about it in his sleep.

"At last," he cried, jumping out of bed one night in his night-shirt and cap.

He searched through his spell books until he found what he was looking for, then he carried it upstairs with him and sat up in bed reading it carefully. Every now and then, he nodded and chuckled to himself, and at last, he lay down and went fast asleep.

Felix spent all the next day preparing and just before midnight he left the house making his way to the border. Luckily there was very little moonlight, but he had to go carefully not to be seen by one of the soldiers.

First, he stood facing one way and held up his arms chanting very quietly to himself. He turned and did the same thing facing the other way. Then he jumped smartly to one side and made his way home chuckling to himself.

The following morning he found he had just been in time. The soldiers were preparing themselves for battle. Rank upon rank were lined up facing each other. Felix was not smiling now. Thinking of all the dreadful things that would have happened if he had not cast his spell made him very angry.

On one side of the border, King Lofty stood near his white horse his captains grouped about him.

King Trump was already astride his black horse waiting for his officers to tell him they were ready.

There were only a few yards between the armies, but when Felix thought of those few yards he had to smile. He went out and sat on a large rock where he could see everything that was going on. He did not want to miss anything.

Felix had to admit they looked a wonderful sight lined up facing each other. The soldiers stood in ranks, their spears and shields glinting in the sun. Behind them the archers stood, their bows and arrows ready.

Now, both kings held their swords aloft ready to give a signal. Both arms came down almost at the same moment. The two armies marched towards each other, shields in place and spears ready. Both sides thrust their spears forward but they did not touch the men on the other side. Instead they buckled and snapped in half! The soldiers fell backwards in a heap. The same thing happened to the next rank and the one after.

By now the archers had started to let fly their arrows. These flew only so far in the air then fell harmlessly to the ground. Felix was enjoying himself, he laughed until the tears ran down his cheeks.

Some of the archers began to smile, then laugh; they could not help it. It was such a funny sight – all those arms and legs waving in the air.

King Lofty and King Trump looked stupidly at their men who kept marching forward and falling on top of the soldiers already on the ground. The laughter spread until even the two kings had to join in. At last, one of the officers gave the command to halt.

Felix waved his arms to take the invisible wall away. One of the soldiers noticed Felix sitting on the rock, and pointed to him. Everybody became silent looking towards him. King Lofty and King Trump rode up to him and dismounted. Seeing his hat and cloak they looked at each other.

"You did this," said King Lofty.

"Why?" asked King Trump.

"Yes, it was me," said Felix. "Why? Well, someone had to do something before you destroyed each other."

"How did you do it?" asked King Lofty.

"It was simple really,' said Felix. "I put an invisible wall between you."

Well, the kings were very impressed and said how clever he had been.

"Yes, I know that," said Felix modestly.

"Come now," he went on. "Shake hands and forget this war. It seems to me that you are both to blame."

The two kings looked at each other. Then they smiled and clasped hands. The soldiers cheered their kings, the officers and most of all Felix, the clever magician.

Felix was delighted his spell had worked. He invited both kings and their officers to his house to rest and talk. All the men of both sides joined together, laughing and clapping each other on the back.

Felix waved his arms, and food and drink appeared by magic. The men cheered once more, then they ate and drank until it was almost dark, before going home. There was so much to tell their families, they could hardly believe all the wonderful things that had happened that day.

Felix's name was on everyone's lips, and he was blessed that day and for many, many years to come.

GLUM THE GIANT

Glum, the Giant, strode along the road away from the village with his bag on his shoulder. He had been shopping. Several people smiled at him but he only nodded back at them. They took no notice, they were used to him.

Then some children followed him chanting,
"There goes poor old Glum,
He has a pain in his tum.
Oh, why does he scowl?
He should be called Growl."

Glum spun round and glared at them. They ran away laughing, as they knew he would not harm them.

Glum went on his way thinking hard. What was the matter with him? Why couldn't he smile and laugh like other people? Perhaps if he tried it would help. How did they smile? They showed their teeth, didn't they? Glum thought he would try out his idea of a smile on the next person he saw.

The giant went on his way until he saw a boy on a horse coming towards him.

"Hello Glum," called the boy. Glum remembered his idea and smiled. At least he thought it was a smile, but it frightened the horse so much that it reared up and bolted almost unseating the boy.

Glum dropped his bag and took only a few strides to catch the horse by the reins, just in time.

"Whoa there," Glum said gently stroking the horse's nose with one finger while he helped the boy to sit up straight. The horse stopped trembling and neighed as if in answer.

"Are you alright, boy?" he asked.

"Yes, thank you," was the rather shaky answer.

"Well, take it easy then, goodbye."

Glum left the boy wondering what could have happened for the giant to pull such a funny face.

Glum came to a large pond where a lot of ducks and fish lived. He leaned over to look into the water but his shadow was so dark that he could not see himself.

Glum still did not know what he looked like.

He carried on until he came to his gloomy old castle and went in slamming the door behind him.

Glum looked about him and seemed to see everything with new eyes. He had never noticed before that the dark grey walls were hanging with cobwebs, or that the floor was so dirty and the furniture thick with dust. He had no one to look after him, it was true.

"That is no excuse," Glum told himself, suddenly upset with the state the place was in.

"I ought to look for a wife, but who would have me? If the castle has to be cleaned I will have to do it myself."

He made himself some supper and went to bed feeling more glum than ever.

That night he had a strange dream. He was a handsome giant who had rescued a fair young giantess from the clutches of her wicked uncle. When he woke he remembered his dream and thought sadly how lonely he was.

"Come on," he reminded himself. "There is work to be done."

All day long he swept, dusted and polished the old castle. Clouds of dust flew out of the doors and all the windows. The people in the village some distance away wondered what on earth was happening.

By the time Glum had finished, the castle looked a different place but he himself was a mess; not that he ever looked very tidy but now he was dirty as well.

He picked up a large bar of soap and a towel as big as a blanket and made his way to the river nearby.

First, he took off his boots, emptied the dust out of them, then polished them with his sleeve until they shone. Then he waded into the river as he was, with his clothes on and sat in the middle of it.

"Ah," he sighed. "That feels nice and cool after all my hard work."

Glum bent forward to splash himself with water, holding the soap in one hand. He stared at the face looking back at him for a few moments, then he began to roar with peals of laughter. He laughed and laughed until the tears rolled down his cheeks.

At last, still chuckling, he looked up to see the people from the village standing on the bank watching him in amazement.

"Are you alright?" one of the men asked him.

Glum laughed again.

"I've just seen the funniest face looking up at me from the river," he explained. "It is the first time I have seen something that made me want to laugh. I do feel good now. I can understand at last why people like to smile and feel happy."

"That was your own face in the water," one little boy said before they could stop him.

"My own face?" Glum sounded astonished. He looked again into the water and saw himself once more.

"Well," he said at last. "If that is what I look like, no wonder I am called Glum."

He put his head under the water and gave himself a good scrub, clothes and all. Then he stood up and shook himself before reaching for his towel.

"I can cut your hair and trim your beard if you would like me to," the barber dared to say.

"Why, that is most kind of you," Glum said smiling at him.

They all smiled back.

"No time like the present," the barber said, taking comb and scissors from his pocket.

When he had finished, everybody stared at Glum.

"There, that has made a difference, hasn't it?" said the barber.

Glum leaned over and looked at himself in the river. He turned his head from side to side, putting his hand up to feel his beard. Then he smiled and at last he laughed showing his white teeth. His hair and beard were brown and his eyes deep blue.

"Is that really me?" he asked.

"Yes, indeed it is," an old lady answered. "If I may say so, you are a very handsome giant now."

Glum rose to his feet and bowed low to her. "Thank you, my lady," he chuckled.

Everybody clapped and laughed. The children danced around him singing,

"Oh me, oh my, what a handsome guy,

He will make all the ladies sigh."

Then Glum thought, maybe some day, his dream might not be so impossible after all.

THE MAGIC COMBS

"King Bonkers may be my father," said Princess Mirabelle, as she brushed the mud from the coat of her little dog, "but I think he must be the silliest King that ever lived."

"King Bonkers may be my husband," said the Queen as she pruned her favourite rose bush, "but I have to agree with you. If he isn't complaining how bored he is, he is playing silly tricks on people. Everybody is tired of him and if he doesn't mend his ways soon, the people will choose a new King and we shall all be turned out of our beautiful palace."

King Bonkers walked across the lawn towards the Queen and Princess.

"I am so bored," he said.

"We could all be bored if we walked around all day doing nothing," said the Queen. "Have you signed your important papers today?"

"No," answered King Bonkers. "Important papers bore me."

"Well, you could help me prune the roses," suggested the Queen.

"No thank you," said King Bonkers, "I might prick my fingers." And he walked out of the palace gate and up the hill to Wizard Winegum's house.

Wizard Winegum wasn't very pleased to see King Bonkers.

"Tell me what you want quickly," he said. "I am very busy today."

"I am bored," said King Bonkers, "and I want a spell to make something exciting happen."

Wizard Winegum stroked his long white beard thoughtfully.

"Well hm, well hm, I have some magic combs," he said. "If you comb your hair with one of these combs, everything you touch for half an hour afterwards will turn into something different."

"Into what?" asked King Bonkers.

"That's the trouble," answered Wizard Winegum. "You won't know until you touch it. The combs are quite expensive. Twenty gold pieces each."

"I will take two," said King Bonkers and he counted out forty gold pieces.

"Are you quite sure you want two?" asked Wizard Winegum, taking the combs down from his high shelf. "Surely one will be enough?"

"I want two," said King Bonkers and he took the combs and ran back to the palace as fast as his little fat legs would carry him.

Puffing and panting he ran up the stairs to the Queen's bedroom. The Queen was sitting at her dressing table brushing her hair.

"I have bought you a nice new comb, dear," said King Bonkers handing her one of the combs.

"Oh thank you, that is kind of you," she said and she combed her hair with the magic comb. She then put the comb down and picked up her hair brush.

As soon as she touched it, the brush turned into a spider. The Queen hated spiders. She screamed and dropped the spider. It fell onto her lap.

She tried to knock the spider from her lap onto the floor but as she touched it, it turned into a mouse. The Queen was terrified of mice. She climbed onto a chair screaming to King Bonkers to take the mouse away.

As she touched the chair it turned into a kangaroo. It hopped out of the door with the Queen clinging to its neck.

Kong Bonkers thought this was very funny and laughed and laughed until the tears ran down his fat cheeks.

Still laughing, King Bonkers went to give the other comb to Princess Mirabelle. The princess was playing with her little dog on her bedroom floor. King Bonkers handed her the comb.

"Oh thank you, father," she said, and combed her hair with the new comb.

She picked up a slide to put in her hair. At once the slide turned into a ginger kitten. The ginger kitten scratched her and wriggled out of her hands. It ran through the bedroom door and down the stairs chased by the princess's little dog.

Princess Mirabelle ran to the door to call her dog back. As she touched the door it turned into a horse. The horse ran down the stairs after the dog and the kitten.

Soon the whole palace was in an uproar with the kangaroo, dog, horse, kitten and mouse all chasing each other.

King Bonkers hadn't had so much fun for years. He laughed and laughed until he thought his sides would burst.

The next morning, King Bonkers left the palace bright and early to buy two more magic combs from Wizard Winegum.

Princess Mirabelle watched him from her bedroom window. She felt sure he was up to no good and had something to do with what had happened the day before. She decided to follow him.

She crouched down outside Wizard Winegum's door and listened through the keyhole as King Bonkers told the Wizard how pleased he had been with the combs and that he wanted to buy two more.

Princess Mirabelle ran back to the palace and told the Queen all she had overheard.

The Queen was very angry. "King Bonkers needs to be taught a lesson he will not forget in a hurry," she said. She bent down and whispered something in Princess Mirabelle's ear.

Princess Mirabelle smiled as she and the Queen went into the bedroom. They both sat down in front of the Queen's dressing table and started to brush their hair.

King Bonkers was very pleased to see them together when he entered the bedroom. It would save him a walk. He gave them a comb each and sat down on the Queen's bed to wait for the fun to begin.

After thanking him politely, the Queen and the Princess combed their hair with the magic combs AND THEN stood up together and walked slowly over to King Bonkers. The Queen put out her hand and touched King Bonkers on the top of his bald head.

King Bonkers turned into a big, fat round ball.

"Oh look!" said the Queen to Princess Mirabelle. "What a pretty ball. Throw it out of the window and see how well it bounces."

"Oh NO NO NO. I'm not a ball I'm ME!" shouted King Bonkers, but the Queen and the Princess pretended not to hear him.

Princess Mirabelle picked up the ball and at once the King turned into a frog.

"What a horrid frog," said the Queen. "Give it to me and I will put it in the fish pond."

"No, no. I'm not a frog, please don't put me in the fish pond. I can't swim," pleaded the King.

Between them the Queen and Princess Mirabelle soon turned King Bonkers into so many different things he felt quite giddy.

At last he turned into a little bird and flew out of the window and hid himself in a large oak tree.

"Oh dear, oh dear," he said. "I am so dizzy with all this changing. I haven't enjoyed it at all. I will never again use magic to play silly tricks on people." As he spoke, King Bonkers turned back into a King once more. He was a very fat king so it took him a long time to climb down from the tree.

"Oh dear, oh dear," he thought. "I do hope nobody sees me. It is so undignified for a *King* to have to climb down from a tree."

On reaching the ground he looked carefully around but fortunately no one was in sight. Full of his new resolve, he quickly returned to the palace and it wasn't long before he was renowned for his wisdom and good sense.